SECRET of the WINGS

Adapted by Lisa Marsoli

Illustrated by the Disney Storybook Artists

A GOLDEN BOOK • NEW YORK

Copyright © 2012 Disney Enterprises, Inc. All rights reserved. Published in the United States by Golden Books, an imprint of Random House
Children's Books, a division of Random House, Inc., 1745 Broadway, New York, NY 10019, and in Canada by
Random House of Canada Limited, Toronto, in conjunction with Disney Enterprises, Inc. Golden Books, A Golden Book,
A Big Golden Book, the G colophon, and the distinctive gold spine are registered trademarks of Random House, Inc.

ISBN: 978-0-7364-3003-6
randomhouse.com/kids
Printed in the United States of America
10 9 8 7 6 5 4 3 2 1

Tinkers' Nook was bustling with activity. The tinker fairies were making snowflake baskets for the fairies of winter.

A flock of snowy owls soon arrived for the baskets, bringing a final shipment order for Fairy Mary with them.

"Goodness," Fairy Mary said. "They need twenty more baskets for tomorrow's pickup!"

Tink watched as the magnificent birds headed off toward the Winter Woods. "There's a whole other world over there," she said to herself.

Later that day, Tink volunteered to help her friend
Fawn take animals to the Winter Woods to hibernate.
But Fawn told Tink that they could only bring animals
to the border, and weren't allowed to go into the Winter
Woods. Then she got distracted by a sleeping marmot.

"No hibernating yet!" she called into the animal's ear.
"You do that in winter!"

Even though she knew it could be dangerous, Tink
was very curious about the Winter Woods. With Fawn
distracted, Tinker Bell jumped across the border!

Tink gazed in wonder at the beautiful wintry landscape, enchanted by the delicate snowflakes that drifted down all around her.

Suddenly, her wings began to sparkle in a burst of colorful light—and she heard the faint sound of a baby's laugh!

The magical moment ended when Fawn yanked
Tinker Bell back into autumn. Fawn touched Tink's
wings and gasped. They were freezing!
Fawn rushed Tink straight to the fairy hospital.
A healing-talent fairy examined Tink's wings. Then she
warmed them until they were back to normal again.

Tink was on a mission to find out what had made her wings sparkle. She flew off to the Book Nook, where she found a wing-shaped book she hoped would give her some answers. Unfortunately, a bookworm had chewed through the pages!

A fairy told Tink that the author of the book—the Keeper—might be able to help her. But he lived in the Winter Woods.

Tinker Bell put on a warm outfit, packed the book in a bag, and snuck into the tinkers' workshop. Then the adventurous fairy climbed inside a snowflake basket. Tink's fairy friends watched closely.

In a moment, Tink was soaring through the air. The young owl that had picked up the basket had no idea there was a stowaway inside!

As the owl crossed into the Winter Woods, Tinker Bell
felt a cold blast of air. She peeked out of the basket and saw
a majestic valley spread before her!

Suddenly, the owl accidentally let go of Tink's basket! She crashed onto the landing area, sending snowflakes scattering everywhere.

Tinker Bell ducked behind the basket to hide—then realized that her book had been flung onto the ice. She had to get it back before a winter fairy found it!

Just then, Lord Milori, the Lord of Winter, arrived.
"Now, that is odd," he said, grabbing the book from
Sled, a winter fairy who had spotted it. Lord Milori
asked Sled to return the book to the Keeper.

Tinker Bell secretly followed Sled to the Hall of Winter. When she arrived, she spotted the Keeper, whose name was Dewey. Then another winter fairy rushed into the room and asked Dewey why her wings were sparkling!

Suddenly, Tinker Bell's wings began to sparkle, too—just like when she had crossed the border the other day! An irresistible force pulled her toward the fairy. The fairy's name was Periwinkle.

The girls hoped Dewey could explain what was happening to their wings. He brought Tink and Peri over to a giant snowflake.

"Just put your wings into the light," he told them.

A few seconds later, the chamber filled with images showing the journey of a baby's first laugh—a laugh that split in two and landed on a dandelion!

One half traveled to the Pixie Dust Tree on the warm side of Pixie Hollow, and Tinker Bell was born. The other half blew into the Winter Woods, and baby Periwinkle arrived.

That meant Tink and Peri were sisters!

Suddenly, Lord Milori arrived. He was concerned about the book Sled had found. "What if a warm fairy brought it here?" he asked Dewey. "If a warm fairy comes here, you *will* send them back."

Peri and Tink, who had been hiding behind the snowflake, gasped. Did this mean that Tinker Bell would have to go home already?

Dewey told the girls they could have a little time to visit before Tink had to go home. Tink put on her coat and earmuffs to keep warm.

When they got to Periwinkle's house, Peri showed Tink a bundle of items she had been collecting.

"You collect Lost Things, too?" asked Tink.

"I call them Found Things," Periwinkle replied, smiling.

Next, they went to the Frost Forest, where Peri introduced Tinker Bell to her friends Gliss and Spike. They went ice-sliding, which was like sledding on a frozen roller coaster. Tink had a wonderful time!

That night outside Periwinkle's house, after Tinker Bell had built a fire to stay warm, she had a thought.

"I made it warmer over here," she said. "Maybe I could make it colder over there." Tink wanted her sister to be able to visit her on the warm side of Pixie Hollow.

Suddenly, the snow floor crumbled beneath them. It was melting from the fire! A lynx brought them to safety. Dewey told the girls that now it was *really* time for Tink to go back home.

The girls realized that they might never see each other again. Tinker Bell had to come up with a plan.

When the three fairies reached the border, Tinker Bell broke into fake sobs.

"I can't watch!" Dewey cried.

"Meet me here tomorrow. There's something I need you to bring," Tink whispered to Peri.

A little while later, Tinker Bell arrived back on the warm side of Pixie Hollow. She asked her friends Clank and Bobble for help.

The three fairies were hard at work when a few of Tinker Bell's other friends stopped by. Clank had told them about Tink's newfound sister, and everyone couldn't wait to find out more about her!

The next day, Tinker Bell arrived at the border with Bobble and Clank, who were pulling a strange-looking contraption. It was a snowmaker!

Periwinkle and her friends gasped in surprise.

"How does it work?" Peri asked.

A few seconds later, the snowmaker started
to grate a block of ice and turn it into snow.
Peri was delighted!

Peri's journey through the warm seasons was filled with one amazing sight after the next. She saw a fast-moving rainbow and a field of blooming flowers. She thought everything was so beautiful!

Soon, Fawn, Iridessa, Rosetta, Silvermist, and Vidia
got to meet the frost fairy face to face.

"Everyone . . . this is Periwinkle, my sister!" Tinker
Bell announced.

Peri was continuing her tour of the warm side of Pixie Hollow when Tink noticed that Peri's wings had started to wilt. The snowmaker was running out of ice, and there wasn't enough snow to keep Peri cold!

Immediately, Tink brought Peri back to the border.

At that moment, Lord Milori appeared. "Lift your wings," he told Peri. "Let the cold surround them."

Suddenly, Queen Clarion, the Queen of Pixie Hollow, arrived. She looked at the girls sadly.

"This is why we do not cross the border," Lord Milori told Tinker Bell and Periwinkle. "I'm sorry. You two may never see each other again."

As the girls went their separate ways, Lord Milori mounted his owl and flew off—but not before he knocked the snowmaker into a stream.

Instead of going over the waterfall as Lord Milori had intended, the contraption caught on a ledge. There it remained, making a snowstorm out of the ice chunks that flowed into it!

Later that day, Queen Clarion tried to make Tinker Bell understand why the rule about not crossing the border was so important. She told the story of two fairies who fell in love. One was from the warm seasons and one was from the Winter Woods. One of the fairies crossed the border and broke a wing—an injury for which there was no cure.

Just as the queen finished her sad tale, it began to snow!

Queen Clarion was concerned. It was very dangerous for snow to fall in Pixie Hollow.

Queen Clarion, Tink, and a group of fairies arrived at the stream to find Clank and Bobble attempting to free the snowmaker—which was making a small blizzard—from the ledge.

Everyone rushed to help. Finally, they succeeded in pushing the machine into the water, but snow still showered down from the sky!

"It's too late," Queen Clarion said quietly. "The seasons have been thrown out of balance."

If the warm side got too cold, the Pixie Dust Tree would freeze—and there would never be any more pixie dust. Just then, Tink noticed that a flower that Periwinkle had brought to the warm side of Pixie Hollow was still blooming!

Tinker Bell flew straight to the Winter Woods, but her wings iced over and she fell. She asked why the flower was still alive. Gliss explained that frost tucks warm air inside.

"We could frost the Pixie Dust Tree before the freeze hits it," Peri suggested.

Tink and the frost fairies flew to the Pixie Dust Tree. They got right to work, but it looked as if the job would be too big for them to complete in time.

Then Tink spotted Dewey, Lord Milori, and the rest of the frost fairies flying toward them.

But Tink was afraid that help had come too late. The freeze had already swept across the warm seasons of Pixie Hollow and the Pixie Dust Tree.

The fairies gathered anxiously around the Pixie Dust Well. Sunlight was streaming through the frozen branches of the tree. Ever so slowly, the frost melted. Then the pixie dust began to flow again!

All of a sudden, Tinker Bell realized that she had broken a wing when she had flown to the Winter Woods.

"It's getting warmer," Tink said bravely to Peri. "You should get back to winter."

As the sisters held hands and said good-bye, an explosion of light burst from their wings. Magically, Tink's wing was healed!

From that day on, warm fairies could cross over the border into winter anytime they liked. A coat of frost kept them safe and warm. Friendships between warm fairies and winter fairies bloomed—all just as beautiful as Periwinkle's flower!